FULL MOUSE EMPTY MOUSE

Published by
M A G I N A T I O N   P R E S S
An Educational Publishing Foundation Book
American Psychological Association
750 First Street, NE
Washington, DC 20002

For more information about our books, including a complete catalog, please write to us, call 1-800-374-2721, or visit our website at www.maginationpress.com.

Editor: Darcie Conner Johnston
Project Coordinator: Becky Shaw
Design production by Susan K. White
Printed by Worzalla, Stevens Point, Wisconsin

Library of Congress Cataloging-in-Publication Data

Zeckhausen, Dina.
Full mouse, empty mouse : a tale of food and feelings / written by Dina Zeckhausen ;
illustrated by Brian Boyd.
p. cm.
Summary: Two mice starve or stuff themselves in response to upset feelings,
until they learn healthier ways to express them. Includes extensive information
for parents on eating disorders prevention.
ISBN-13: 978-1-4338-0132-7 (hardcover : alk. paper)
ISBN-10: 1-4338-0132-9 (hardcover : alk. paper)
ISBN-13: 978-1-4338-0133-4 (pbk. : alk. paper)
ISBN-10: 1-4338-0133-7 (pbk. : alk. paper)
1. Compulsive eating—Juvenile literature. 2. Eating disorders—Juvenile literature.
3. Eating disorders in children—Prevention. I. Boyd, Brian, 1955-. II. Title.

RC552.C65Z35 2007
616.85'26—dc22   2007020630

10 9 8 7 6 5 4 3 2 1

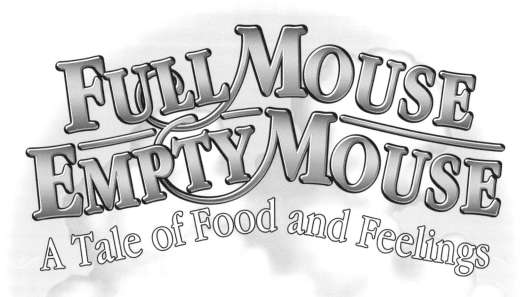

FULL MOUSE EMPTY MOUSE

A Tale of Food and Feelings

written by Dina Zeckhausen, Ph.D.
illustrated by Brian Boyd

MAGINATION PRESS • WASHINGTON, DC

In a time that's right around today,

    And a place that's not too far away,

        In an old brick house with climbing trees,

            Where lacy curtains catch the breeze,

A family lived without a trace,
And here our Mousey Tale takes place.
The Squeaks would sneak throughout the house,
But never leave a trace of mouse.

The Grumble clan was unaware

That mousey folks were living there.

The Squeaks crept deep beneath the floors,

Between the walls, behind the doors.

The Grumbles never got a peek...

...Until a game of hide-and-seek!

Billy Blue and Sally Rose

Played hide-and-seek on tippy-toes.

Best hiding place for Billy Blue?

Why, inside Mr. Grumble's shoe!

Sally Rose preferred his sock,

Or just behind the Grumble clock.

W hen Mr. Grumble found this out,

    He stomped his foot and gave a shout.

"The Grumbles will search high and low!

    Those nasty mice have got to go!"

Mr. Grumble set up traps,

    One with glue and one that snaps.

The Grumble boy would grab a broom,
    And chase the mice from room to room.
They put the hound dog on the case.
    His favorite game was sniff-and-chase.
The cat was now in on the deal,
    And hungry for a mousey meal.
With cat and trap and broom and hound,
    The mice were now on shaky ground.

Afraid their children might get hurt,
The Squeaks remained on high alert.
Mr. Squeak worked through the night
To make sure they would be all right.
His wife-mouse cleaned from dusk to dawn,
Till every trace of mouse was gone.

The two kid-mice loved Mom and Dad,
And did not want them to feel bad.
They both agreed the way to cope
Was "don't complain or whine or mope."
They stayed alert, hid high on shelves,
And kept their feelings to themselves.

Billy tried to hide his fear,
And so he never cried a tear.
He sat alone on the windowsill,
And tried to be completely still.
He calmed his nervous tummy down
With little bits of food he found.
He ate and watched the cat for hours,
Or stared at Mrs. Grumble's flowers.

He wished that other mice could know
The feelings he tried not to show.
But mice at school said he was *fat!*
And too slow to outrun the cat.
The teasing caused his heart to ache,
And made him want to eat more cake.
The pain inside him grew and grew,
But other mice, they never knew.

Sally Rose did the reverse—

Avoiding food—but she felt worse!

Fearing danger behind every door,

She moved and moved, then moved some more.

"Perhaps if I am small," thought she,

"I'll be as safe as I can be.

And maybe if I disappear,

No cat or dog will find me here."

Sally's body grew too thin,

But it turned out that thin was "in."

So other mice said she looked *great!*

While Sally pushed away her plate.

But as she turned to skin and bone,

She spent more of her time alone.

The pain inside her grew and grew,

But other mice, they never knew.

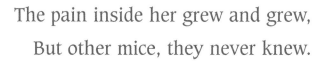

14

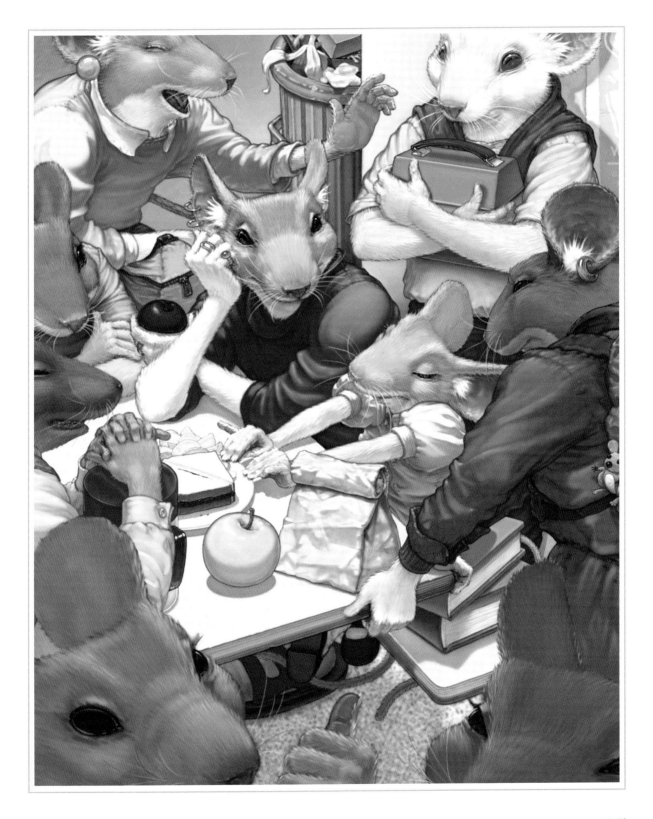

The Squeaks did not know what to do
About Sally Rose and Billy Blue.
While Billy's pants were growing tight,
He asked his Mom for one more bite.
She tried to find some helpful words,
And worried as he reached for thirds.

ally would not eat her fill,

And never let herself sit still.

Full mouse? Empty mouse? Signals crossed,

And all the Squeaks felt very lost.

Family meals once filled the heart,

But now the Squeaks felt far apart.

One day wise old Aunt Louise,
While nibbling on a bit of cheese,
Heard Billy Blue and Sally Rose
No longer fit into their clothes!

18

She wondered if they were all right,
And invited them upstairs that night.
With goose bumps underneath their hairs,
They carefully snuck up the stairs.

In Aunt Lou's lap, the mice were sure
    Their secrets were safe and secure.
  She listened close and held them tight,
    And as the moon lit up the night,
  They let out all they'd held inside.
    With sweet relief, the two mice cried.

Once their tale was crystal clear,
    Lou spoke the words they longed to hear.
  "You two have tried so hard to be
    A big help to your family.
  You thought that hiding all your stress
    Would help your parents worry less.
  But ignoring what your insides said
    Only made things worse instead."

21

"Your body speaks with a sensation
That gives important information.
Tummy and Heart live right next door.
Find out what each is asking for."

"First, let's talk about your Heart.
It plays a truly vital part.
Your Heart feels things that must be shared,
Like happy, angry, sad, and scared.
Don't ignore them, don't conceal.
Show and tell the things you feel."

"Your Tummy also has a pull.
It says it's hungry or it's full.
If you eat too little or too much,
You'll find it hard to stay in touch
With feelings coming from your Heart.
Let "full" and "hungry" do their part
To help you eat just what you should,
Because starved and stuffed do not feel good!"

"Eating right will make you strong,
  Your eyes will shine, your fur grow long,
  Your body will be full of life,
  Your mind as sharp as any knife!"

"The way for you to be your best?
  Get your Heart's words off your chest.
  Trust your family, don't pretend,
  For love will be there in the end."

Your Mom and Daddy really care,

So in the morning try to share

Those things you feel but do not show.

Your Dad and Mommy need to know."

The two mice snuck back to their bed,

And dreamed of what their aunt had said.

When they awoke to morning birds,

And recalled their Auntie's words,

They ate breakfast in a happy mood,

And chose the right amount of food.

They cleaned their dishes, made their bed,
Then Billy got real brave and said,
"Hey, Mom and Dad, is it okay
To tell you how we feel today?"
Their Mommy said, "Why, yes, my dears,
What's up with you? We are all ears!"

And so the mice began to chat
Of close calls with the scary cat,
Of how they feared their certain doom
When Boy just missed them with the broom,
Of being teased and tummy aches,
Of loneliness and food mistakes.
They said they thought they'd had enough
Of feeling starved and feeling stuffed.

Their Mom and Daddy stroked their fur,
And told them both how proud they were.
"Don't keep your feelings to yourself.
We love you more than cheese itself!"

Now Bill and Sally ask themselves,
"Full Mouse? Empty Mouse? Something else?"
The answers aren't too hard to read.
Their bodies tell them what they need.

With Tummy and Heart they stay in touch.
They eat enough, but not too much.
They talk about the way they feel,
And now they love their family meal!

The Squeaks spend time out in the breeze.

They smell the air, and climb the trees.

The family loves to take a break,

And catch big tadpoles at the lake.

They feel carefree and laugh out loud

When finding mouse-shapes in a cloud.

The more time spent as family,

The better life turns out to be.

You'll never hear a Grumble shriek

About a game of hide-and-seek.

The Grumbles stopped the man-mouse wars

When mousey games were moved outdoors.

Now all is peaceful once again

Inside the house of mice and men.

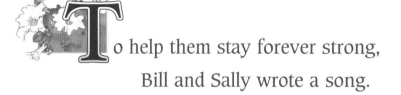To help them stay forever strong,
Bill and Sally wrote a song.

Listen to your body.
  It's not too hard to read.
Go inside and you will find
  The answers that you need.

To find out what you're feeling,
  Here's the place to start:
Understand the language
  Of your Tummy and your Heart.

Speak up if you're angry,
  Get a hug if you feel scared,
And if you're sad, just cry those tears,
  'Cause feelings should be shared!

Sally Rose and Billy Blue
    Were two kids just like me and you.
They grew up to be amazing mice,
        So here's a bit of good advice:

Eat when you feel hungry,
    And stop when you are full.
Your body's just a small part
    Of what makes you beautiful!

Listen to your body.
    It's not too hard to read.
Go inside and you will find
    The answers that you need.

Note to Parents

For both adults and children, eating is not always governed by rational choices. Deeper hidden needs play a significant role. Without our full awareness, our relationship with food is linked with how we manage, reject, or numb our feelings, how we communicate with others, and how we feel about ourselves. Food is not as simple as we think.

To complicate matters, the food industry, the diet industry, the fashion industry, and the medical establishment shower us with often conflicting messages about health and beauty. Separating the facts from the fads is not an easy task. Even when we know which choices are healthy, large measures of discipline or courage may be needed to overcome our habits, desires, and fears.

In the meantime, the rates of obesity and other forms of disordered eating are climbing. Since the 1970s, the percentage of overweight children and adolescents in the United States has more than doubled. The American Academy of Pediatrics now states that the prevalence of overweight among children has reached epidemic proportions. At the same time, studies show that 40 to 60 percent of fourth graders have poor body image and have engaged in dieting behavior. Research indicates that dieting in children can actually lead to weight *gain*. For other children, dieting can be the beginning of the slippery slope into anorexia and bulimia. According to the National Institute of Mental Health, the death rate among people with anorexia is 12 times higher than the annual death rate due to all causes among females ages 15 to 24. With so much at stake, it is essential that we become more aware of early vulnerabilities and warning signs, and that we learn how to support our children who may be at risk.

Nutrition and exercise are crucial for healthy physical development. However, focusing solely on them misses a fundamental point about the powerful human connection to food: Psychology plays a literally scale-tipping role. With this in mind, *Full Mouse, Empty Mouse* was written as a prevention tool. Its purpose is to help young children begin to identify and sort out the messages their bodies are sending, to separate "feelings" messages from "food" messages. Its goal is to encourage the healthy expression of feelings, and a healthy connection between mind and body. The ability to listen to our bodies, and to accurately translate and respond to their messages, is essential for preventing eating disorders—and for our overall well-being.

EXPRESSING FEELINGS THROUGH TALK

In *Full Mouse, Empty Mouse*, Billy Blue and Sally Rose try to deal with their anxiety and loneliness through food—by stuffing or by starving—until they learn better coping skills from their family. The first step, they find, is to listen to the body and distinguish the language of the tummy from the language of the heart. It is fundamentally important that children learn to recognize these two sets of messages and know how to respond to each.

It may be helpful to talk with young children in these terms, as they are used in this story. The language of the tummy is straightforward: It says "hungry" or "full." The language of the heart includes our entire range of feelings: happy, sad, scared, lonely, bored, excited, frustrated, satisfied, tired, energetic, angry, nervous, relieved, and more. When the tummy says "hungry," it's time to eat; when it says "full," it's time to stop. And when the heart talks, it's time for such things as words, hugs, and tears.

- **Talk About Talking**
  Help your children understand the importance of expressing feelings directly, instead of through indirect ways such as food. As Aunt Louise says in this story, when we're having stressful feelings, talking about those feelings is one of the best ways to feel better. Sometimes just getting them off your chest helps. Sometimes knowing that someone else cares is all you need. And sometimes another person can help you come up with solutions to problems or inspire you to action. We don't have to know exactly what we're feeling before we start to talk. In fact, confiding itself can help us make sense of our feelings. And confiding helps us feel connected to each other, which is essential to happiness. As a springboard to talking with children, parents might find the Discussion Questions following this Note to be helpful.

- **Provide an Opening**
  Help children get into the habit of sharing feelings and thoughts by offering gentle prompts. For

example, you might say, "I have a feeling you had a hard time at school today. Would you like to talk about it?" or "I can tell you were upset by that. I would have felt the same way" or "I'll bet that made you angry. Most kids would have been mad if that had happened to them."

- **Listen to Your Child**
  Pick a time for conversation when you aren't in a rush or distracted. Give children your full attention, let them talk, listen as much as you can without advising, and give them "permission" to have and express a full range of feelings without judging or minimizing any of them. For example, it's normal and healthy for boys to feel sadness or fear, just as girls can feel angry.

- **Offer Food Appropriately**
  Avoid offering comfort to your children through food. At the same time, resist responding to your own feelings with food, as children often follow a parent's example.

- **Avoid Telling Too Much**
  It is appropriate for children to share any feelings with parents, but the reverse is not true. Use care when disclosing information to children, and keep expressions of feelings mild or gently instructive. Inappropriate or intense disclosures can be distressing and potentially damaging.

- **Encourage Ties**
  Encourage children to think about the other caring adults in their lives whom they can trust to confide in. These would include other family members, teachers, and family friends. Older siblings can also be a tremendous asset. The more loving bonds your child forms, the better for his or her health and comfort.

- **Include Other Outlets**
  Writing about feelings is another direct outlet for verbalizing them. Keeping a journal, writing stories or essays, and writing letters are all constructive ways of expressing and clarifying feelings, especially for less gregarious children. Drawing and painting can also be helpful and calming.

THE ROLE OF THE BODY

The relationship between the mind and the body is intricate. Physical activity is vital not only for a healthy body but also for a healthy mind. Exercise is well known to produce body chemicals that elevate mood and maintain a sense of energy and well-being. This may help explain why it's possible to confuse our heart signals with tummy signals: When we feel bad, we sense that if we do *something* with the body, we'll feel better.

- **Listen to the Body**
  Encourage your child to think about what his or her body really needs when he or she feels lonely, scared, bored, angry, frustrated, or sad. You might say, for example, "You ate lunch about an hour ago, so your tummy should still be pretty full. I wonder if your heart is trying to tell you something?" or "It's time for dinner and you didn't have a snack after school, so it's been a while since you ate. I wonder why you don't feel hungry. Do you think your heart is trying to tell you something?"

- **Make Activity a Habit**
  Encourage children to move their bodies every day. Being active makes you strong and healthy, and it makes you feel good. Encourage sports, both team and individual. Ride bikes as a family, and take walks instead of driving when you can. Visit parks and playgrounds. Set up a basketball hoop or tetherball or play structure in the yard. Visit the swimming pool. Go camping. Take the stairs instead of the elevator. And on the flip side, limit sedentary TV viewing, video games, and computer use.

- **Take a Nap**
  When tired, it's best to rest, even if for a few minutes. Avoid giving your child or yourself a false energy boost with sugar or caffeine.

- **Be an Example**
  If you follow the same guidelines you set for your children, those guidelines will be much easier to implement. And you'll feel better too!

- **Do It for the Right Reasons**
  Communicate the attitude to your children that physical activity is worthwhile for its own sake. It's fun. It lifts the spirit, and it helps us feel alive. We move so that our minds and bodies are functioning optimally, not because we want to look the way we think people want us to look or we need to compensate for calories consumed. Talk about activity in terms of pleasure, rather than anxiety or guilt.

A FEW REMINDERS

1 If your child has recently gained or lost a noticeable amount of weight, take him or her to the doctor. You will want to make sure there are no underlying medical causes.

2 Respect the power of heredity. Before you overreact to your child's body size, review his or her genetic heritage—the sizes of the people on both sides of the family.

3 An increased appetite or weight gain may simply signify an impending growth spurt. Many children grow into their weight if left to their own devices. Meanwhile, children who diet are at greater risk of eating disorders in the future: binge eating, anorexia, or bulimia.

4 Help your child recognize and appreciate the natural diversity of body shapes and sizes.

5 Challenge the "thin" message promoted by society through your words and actions. Emphasize health over thinness. A positive body image protects a child from engaging in dangerous dieting practices.

6 If your child is thinner than average, de-emphasize his or her size. Thin children receive so much praise they may fear the weight gain that accompanies normal physical development. Help your child develop a sense of worth that is based on inner qualities.

7 Never say anything unkind to anyone about his or her body—including yourself.

Discussion Questions

Billy Blue and Sally Rose Squeak were feeling lots of stress.

Q What is stress? What feelings are stress feelings?
A *Stress is what we feel when we're in any situation that is upsetting or challenging. Some stress feelings are fear, worry, loneliness, frustration, anger, confusion, helplessness, embarrassment, and sadness. Stressful situations can last a short time, like forgetting today's homework or losing something you love or arguing with your best friend. Or they can go on for awhile, like going through your parents' divorce or being a bully's favorite target at school.*

Q What caused Billy Blue and Sally Rose to feel stressed?
A *The Grumbles were trying to get rid of them! Billy Blue and Sally Rose were in danger, and they felt frightened and upset.*

Q What are some events and situations you can think of that can cause stress?

Stress can't be ignored. Our bodies, minds, and hearts always try to do something about it.

Q What did Billy Blue do when the Grumbles started to chase him?
A *He ate too much food, trying to comfort himself, and he ignored his tummy when it said "full." He stopped moving his body in order to feel safe. But he found that the less he moved, the worse his body felt.*

Q What happened with Billy's body?
A *He had less energy. His tummy ached. He started to weigh too much, and that was not healthy.*

Q What happened with Billy's mind? What kinds of things did he think?
A *All he thought about was food. This kept his mind off his stress, but there was no room left in his mind to think normal mouse-thoughts.*

Q What happened in Billy's heart? How did he feel?
A *Feeling stuffed was such a strong feeling that it made his other feelings—anger, fear, sadness, and even happiness—disappear.*

Q What happened with Billy's friends?

His friends noticed that he was getting bigger, and they started talking about his body. They did not understand Billy's problem because he hid his feelings inside. The lonelier he became, the more he used food to try to feel better.

Q What happened with Billy's family?

His parents noticed that he was eating too much, and they were worried. Even though they loved him more than cheese itself, they didn't know how to help him because they didn't know what was going on inside.

Q What did Sally Rose do when the Grumbles started to chase her?

She ate too little food, thinking that if she was smaller she would be safer, and she ignored her tummy when it told her it was empty. She moved her body all the time because she was so nervous.

Q What happened to Sally's body?

She had less energy because she didn't have enough food. Her tummy ached because it was hungry. She started to weigh too little, and that was not healthy.

Q What happened with Sally's mind? What kinds of things did she think?

She thought that if she ate less and got smaller and kept moving, she would be safer. She wasn't able to think clearly, or to think normal mouse-thoughts anymore.

Q What happened in Sally's heart? How did she feel?

Sally worried so much there wasn't room for any other feelings—anger, sadness, and even happiness. She even worried so much that she ignored her tummy when it said it was empty.

Q What happened with Sally's friends?

Her friends noticed that she was getting smaller, and they started talking about her body. They did not understand Sally's problem, because she hid her feelings. The lonelier she became, the more she starved herself to try to feel better.

Q What happened with Sally's family?

Her parents noticed that she was not eating enough, and they were worried. Even though they loved her as much as cheese itself, they didn't know how to help her because they didn't realize what was going on inside.

Too much food or too little food didn't help Billy Blue or Sally Rose feel better. But there are other things we can do to help stress feelings go away.

Q What did Billy Blue and Sally Rose do after they talked to Aunt Louise?

They started to talk about all of the feelings that they were keeping inside.

Q Did they feel better?

Yes, they felt much better!

Q What happened after they talked to their parents? What did they do then?

They listened to their tummies and ate the right amount of food.

They started talking about their feelings with their family.

Their parents understood the problems and could do things to help fix them.

They spent more time being together and enjoying each other.

They spent time outside, moving their bodies and doing things they loved.

Everyone has feelings of sadness, worry, anger, and loneliness from time to time. It's just part of being kids and people.

Q Can you think of a time when you felt upset like Billy Blue or Sally Rose?

Q What did you do to feel better?

Q Did it help?

Q What are some things you think can help in the future?

Resources

American Dietetic Association
The American Dietetic Association is the leading national organization of food and nutrition professionals. The ADA maintains a website whose stated purpose is "to serve the public by promoting optimal nutrition, health, and well-being."
www.eatright.org

Dads & Daughters
This organization supports father-daughter relationships and actively addresses cultural and media issues. Their mission is "to make the world safe and fair for our daughters." Their newsletter, *Daughters*, provides information, guidance, and support for raising strong, self-confident girls.
www.dadsanddaughters.org

Eating Disorder Referral and Information Center
The Eating Disorder Referral and Information Center offers information and resources about eating disorders, and referrals to eating disorders professionals around the country.
www.edreferral.com

Eating Disorders Information Network
The Eating Disorders Information Network is dedicated to the prevention of eating disorders through outreach, education, and activism. Among their school and community outreach efforts are the "M.O.D. Squad" (Moms of Daughters) program to assist parents, and the elementary school prevention program "Love Your Body Week," which is based on the book *Full Mouse, Empty Mouse.*
www.myedin.org

Gurze Books
Gurze Books is a publisher that specializes in resources addressing body image, obesity, and eating disorders.
www.gurze.com

Mind on the Media
Sponsors of "Turn Beauty Inside Out Day," this group promotes healthy body image and challenges depictions of girls and women in the media.
www.mindonthemedia.com

National Eating Disorders Association
The National Eating Disorders Association is a nonprofit organization devoted to the prevention and elimination of eating disorders and body dissatisfaction through education, advocacy, and research.
www.nationaleatingdisorders.org

About the Author

DINA ZECKHAUSEN, Ph.D., is the founder and executive director of the Eating Disorders Information Network. She has developed a broad range of school and community-based prevention and awareness programs that have been adopted throughout the United States, and she is a featured expert in the national media on the topic of eating disorders. Dr. Zeckhausen maintains a private practice in Atlanta, Georgia, specializing in the treatment of eating disorders affecting both children and adults.

About the Illustrator

BRIAN BOYD is a painter, illustrator, and designer whose work includes advertising, landscapes, and portraiture, as well as editorial illustration and children's books. He lives and works in Toronto.